BEHIND THE NEWS

RACE AND CRIME

Philip Steele

CRABTREE
Publishing Company
www.crabtreebooks.com

Crabtree Publishing Company

www.crabtreebooks.com

1-800-387-7650

Published in Canada
616 Welland Ave.
St. Catharines, ON
L2M 5V6

Published in the United States
PMB 59051, 350 Fifth Ave.
59th Floor,
New York, NY

Published in 2017 by CRABTREE PUBLISHING COMPANY.

First published in 2014 by Wayland
(A division of Hachette Children's Books)
Copyright © Wayland 2014

Author: Philip Steele

Contributing writer and indexer: Janine Deschenes

Editors: Emma Marriott, Jon Richards, Kathy Middleton, and Janine Deschenes

Designer: Malcolm Parchment

Proofreader: Wendy Scavuzzo

**Production coordinator
and prepress technician:** Ken Wright

Print coordinator: Katherine Berti

Printed in Canada/072016/PB20160525

Photographs and reproductions:
Alamy: © Richard Milnes: p27;

AP Images: Todd McInturf: p4;

Dreamstime: © Rrodrickbeiler : front cover (top);
© Chrisharvey: pp 3 (bottom right), 8;
© Americanspirit: p17 (top); © Angela Ravaioli: p 24;
© Digikhmer: p 42;

Getty Images: © JOSHUA LOTT/Reuters/Corbis p 5

iStock: © ginosphotos: p 15;

Keystone: © Joseph M. Eddins Jr: p 10; © Jeff Malet: p 30

REX: p 20,

Shutterstock: © Turkbug: front cover; © Americanspirit: front cover; © Joseph Sohm title page (top left), p 14; © David P. Lewis: title page (bottom), p 18; © Nando Machado: p3 (top right); © ChameleonsEye: p 9; © Ira Bostic: p 11; © David P. Lewis: p 18; © 360b: p 19; © Nando Machado: p 21; © miker: p 22; © Kostas Koutsaftikis: p 23; © Ryan Rodrick Beiler: p 25; © Paul McKinnon: p 26; © Ryan Rodrick Beiler: p 28; © Carl Stewart: p 31; © Zoran Karapancev: p 33; © Sam DCruz: p 34; © Everett Collection: p 35; © Gino Santa Maria: p 36; © Rena Schild: p 37; © a katz: p 39; © arindambanerjee: p 41; © s_bukley: p 43; © lcswart: p 45;

Wikimedia: front cover: (bottom left); pp 7, 17 (bottom), 40

All other images by Shutterstock

Cover: Blacklivesmatter protesters at Bernie Sanders rally in Portland, Oregon (bottom left); Neo-Nazis at U.S. Capitol (top); Policewoman taking a report, Los Angeles, California (bottom right)

Library and Archives Canada Cataloguing in Publication

Steele, Philip, 1948-, author
         Race and crime / Philip Steele.

(Behind the news)
Includes index.
Issued in print and electronic formats.
ISBN 978-0-7787-2588-6 (hardback).--
ISBN 978-0-7787-2593-0 (paperback).--
ISBN 978-1-4271-1770-0 (html)

        1. Minorities--Crimes against--Juvenile literature. 2. Crime and race--Juvenile literature. 3. Violent crimes--Juvenile literature. 4. Prejudices--Juvenile literature. 5. Racism--Juvenile literature. I. Title.

HV6250.4.E75S74 2016   j364.3'4   C2016-902554-3
                                                                          C2016-902555-1

Library of Congress Cataloging-in-Publication Data

Names: Steele, Philip, 1948- author.
Title: Race and crime / Philip Steele.
Description: New York : Crabtree Publishing, 2016. | Series: Behind the news | Includes index.
Identifiers: LCCN 2016016654 (print) | LCCN 2016018471 (ebook) | ISBN 9780778725886 (reinforced library binding) | ISBN 9780778725930 (pbk.) | ISBN 9781427117700 (electronic HTML)
Subjects: LCSH: Minorities--Crimes against--Juvenile literature. | Crime and race--Juvenile literature. | Violent crimes--Juvenile literature. | CYAC: Hate crimes--Juvenile literature. | Violent crimes,-Juvenile literature. | Prejudices--Juvenile literature.
Classification: LCC HV6250.4.E75 S74 2016 (print) | LCC HV6250.4.E75 (ebook) | DDC 364.3/4--dc23
LC record available at https://lccn.loc.gov/2016016654

CONTENTS

RACE, CRIME, AND THE LAW

In 2013, Renisha McBride had a car accident in Detroit in the early hours of the morning. A 19-year-old African-American teenager, Renisha had drunk over the legal alcohol limit and clipped a parked car. She went to a nearby house for help. Theodore Wafer, a 54-year-old white man, came to the porch.

Questions of race?

Instead of helping Renisha, Wafer shot and killed her. He claimed the shooting was an accident, and he had feared she was trying to break into his home. Wafer was charged with second-degree (non-premeditated, which means unplanned) murder. Renisha's family and many others believed that racism played a part in her murder.

A woman holds the pamphlet handed out at Renisha's funeral, where her friends and family gathered to celebrate her life.

Demonstrators demanded justice following the death of Renisha McBride, expressing the opinion that her shooting by Theodore Wafer was racially motivated.

What is racism?

Racism is the belief that humans are divided by **race**, that peoples' abilities and traits are determined by their race, and that some races are superior to others. Prosecutor Kym Worthy said that race was not a consideration in the charges brought against Theodore Wafer. A public debate began. Why would Wafer assume that Renisha, a young African-American woman, was a criminal? Was the killing motivated by hatred or by fear based on her race?

Wider issues

The Renisha McBride case was not unique. In fact, news headlines often link the issues of race and crime. This book reveals more about stories in the news and questions some **assumptions**. Are some crimes carried out by one ethnic or racial group more than by others? Who are the perpetrators, and who are the victims? How do policing, poverty, prisons, immigration, and the media contribute to ideas about race and crime?

"... **there is a history of racial disparities in the application of our criminal laws—everything from the death penalty to enforcement of our drug laws. And that ends up having an impact in terms of how people interpret the case.**"

United States president Barack Obama, 2013

RACISM IN HISTORY

Throughout history, humans have moved around the world, encountering other populations and mixing with them. Sometimes this has led to tension or violence. The economics of slavery and the expansion of empires in the 1700s and 1800s resulted in power-based claims that some races were superior to other races.

A monument in Zanzibar, Tanzania, recalls the horrors of the East African slave trade.

• Much like it is today, Europe was multi-ethnic in Roman times. There is evidence that African soldiers were stationed on Hadrian's Wall in northern England, back in 208 B.C.E. The Roman Empire relied on slavery, but this was not based on race. Slaves were often people who were captured during war.

• Anti-Semitism, which is prejudice or hatred toward Jews and their religion, was common in medieval Europe. Mass murder of Jews took place in England in 1190. Jews were expelled from England in 1290, from France in 1394, and from Spain in 1492.

• Across Europe from the 1300s to the 1600s, foreign workers were often killed by angry mobs. This could have been because of job competition or xenophobia, which is the irrational fear of strangers.

• The trade of African slaves grew rapidly in the 1500s. Until the 1800s, European countries shipped millions of Africans across the Atlantic in terrible conditions.

• Even after slavery was abolished (in the British Empire in 1833 and in the United States in 1865), former slaves and their descendants often suffered from poverty and discrimination in the criminal justice system.

• The empires of the 1700s and 1800s encouraged Europeans to regard Asians and Africans as inferior races. As well, millions of Native peoples in North and South America and Australia and Oceania were victims of genocide by white settlers from Europe.

• From 1860 on, there was a belief that human biology determined criminal behavior. Scientists and religious leaders claimed, without evidence, that lower social classes and non-whites were "less evolved" than upper-class whites, and were therefore more likely to become criminals.

• These ideas inspired white supremacists such as the Ku Klux Klan in the United States (reestablished 1915) and the Nazi Party (established 1920) in Germany. Supremacists believe that one ethnic group is superior over others.

• After 1945, a civil rights movement rose in the United States. In South Africa, apartheid laws still segregated races from 1948 until 1994.

From 1933 to 1945, the Nazis murdered millions of Jews, Slavs, **Roma**, and other groups in concentration camps, because they believed those groups were inferior.

MYTHS, FACTS, AND FIGURES

Every newborn baby looks different. Hundreds of thousands of years of **evolution** and successful **adaptation** to global environments has resulted in a variety of skin and hair colors, facial features, and body types. People use these differences in appearance to define "races."

The meaning of race and crime?

All humans are members of the same species. We share more than 99.9 percent of our DNA with each other. This means that differences in genes—the parts of DNA that control our characteristics—between different groups of humans are tiny. "Race" is not a scientifically meaningful term, but it is one of the many ways in which humans have decided to classify each other. In the 19th-century, ideas linked some races to criminal behavior. But, ideas about race and criminal behavior vary with geography and time. In other words, these ideas are made up in response to varying situations.

The ethnic make-up of many cities is very diverse, as shown by the mix of these spectators at the River Thames Festival in London, England. People who identify as the same race can have different ethnic backgrounds, or ethnicities.

*Many police forces around the world have been accused of treating people from non-white ethnic groups more severely, opening them up to accusations of **institutional racism**.*

What is ethnicity?

An individual ethnic group is made up of a group of people who share common **descent**. They may also share a culture, language, religion, specific customs, or traditions. People are not born with these values or practices. Instead, they learn them as they grow up. Within any ethnic group, individual people may hold many different values and beliefs. Believing that all members of any one ethnic group have criminal tendencies is a form of racism.

Crime figures

News headlines often focus on crime, generating fear in the general public. This sometimes leads people to place blame on people they fear for crimes. People who are racist often blame whole ethnic communities for crimes. Fortunately, detailed **statistics** on ethnicity and crime can help us discover the truths behind the headlines, to determine whether any ethnic groups are disproportionately represented as perpetrators or victims of types of crime.

> "So peace does not mean just putting an end to violence or to war, but to all other factors that threaten peace, such as discrimination, such as inequality, poverty."

Aung San Suu Kyi, State Counselor of Myanmar (Burma), Nobel Peace Prize winner

FLORIDA, 2012

Trayvon Martin was a 17-year-old African-American teenager. He lived in Miami Gardens, Florida, with his mother and brother. His parents were divorced, and his father's new partner lived in Sanford, Florida. On February 26, 2012, Trayvon and his father were visiting her home in a housing complex called The Retreat.

Tracy Martin

NEWS FLASH

Location: Sanford, Florida
Date: February 26, 2012
Incident: Homicide
Perpetrator: George Zimmerman (aged 28)
Victim: Trayvon Martin (aged 17)
Outcome: Acquittal

Trayvon's father, Tracy Martin, speaks at the first US Congressional Caucus hearing on the status of Black males in July 2013. He and Trayvon's mother, Sybrina Fulton, are now activists for political change.

Suspicion

George Zimmerman, 28, also lived in The Retreat. George was a Neighborhood Watch representative, and according to police and newspaper reports, he regularly called the police if he saw anyone he thought looked suspicious.

Driving his car around the complex that evening, Zimmerman saw Trayvon Martin coming back from a local shop. He called the police because he thought Martin might be "up to no good." Against advice from the police, Zimmerman followed Martin and confronted him. A fight

followed, and Zimmerman killed Martin with his legally owned pistol. The teenager was unarmed. George Zimmerman was arrested, but released after just five hours. Although it was Zimmerman who had pursued Martin, police said there was no evidence that he was not shooting in self-defense. This was legal under Florida's controversial "Stand Your Ground" law, which allows individuals to defend themselves with deadly force.

A racist killing?

Trayvon Martin's death caused outrage across the United States and accusations of racism. Many people felt that Zimmerman was only suspicious of Martin because he was black. Had an unarmed teenager been killed, just because of an unsupported suspicion?

The Florida governor stepped in and appointed a special prosecutor, who laid charges of second-degree murder and manslaughter against George Zimmerman.

In July 2013, a jury acquitted, or removed the charges from, George Zimmerman. Some people were satisfied with the verdict, agreeing that his actions had been legal. Many others feel a grave injustice had been done, and argue that the case proves that racism is still a major issue in the United States.

> "You can stand your ground if you're white, and you can use a gun to do it. But if you stand your ground with your fists and you're black, you're dead."
>
> David Simon, creator of *The Wire* television series, 2013

Protesters demonstrate in support of Trayvon's family and demand justice for his killing.

HOW USEFUL ARE STATISTICS?

Census statistics and crime surveys provide useful information. They identify all sorts of social problems and help decide strategies for crime prevention and policing. Statistics based on ethnic background are often included in the data.

Checking the figures

To interpret statistics, we need to read the small print and find out which methods were used to gather them. To make comparisons, we must know if crimes have been defined in the same way. Are police methods of recording crimes standardized, or the same across different locations? Are the ethnic categories sometimes too broad to be meaningful? For example "Asian," "White," or "Hispanic" could all include many different ethnic groups of people. Further, the selection of crimes in the statistics might be limited. Statistics might refer to street crimes linked to poverty, for example, but exclude **corporate tax evasion**. It is important to look at the bigger picture, too. Is the overall crime rate falling or rising?

*Police records hold detailed information on people. A United Nations (UN) report suggested that when ethnicity is included, it can discourage racial **stereotyping**.*

DEBATE

Should law enforcement pay most attention to a racial or ethnic group because of what the statistics say?

YES

Focusing on a group that statistically is shown to commit certain crimes will stop crimes before they happen.

NO

Focusing on a specific group is unfair and reinforces harmful stereotypes. There are other factors, such as income or social class, which may contribute to crime.

One of many factors

Many statistics do show a clear connection between some ethnicities and higher rates of crime. This does not mean that one is the cause of the other, because many other factors enter the equation. These might include poverty, social class, education, age, gender, integration into society, or wider political considerations. If we look at crime with too much focus on race, we might be missing other important clues. If migrant workers commit crimes, should we point fingers at their ethnicity or at their social status or poverty level?

Statistics on an ethnic group that show a high conviction rate might suggest that more people from one ethnic group are guilty, but that might be misleading. For example, certain groups of people might not have access to good defense lawyers and are therefore more likely to be convicted. Is the criminal justice system evenhanded, or are prejudiced police, courts, or juries coming down too heavily on one particular group, and therefore skewing the statistics?

CRIMINAL JUSTICE STATISTICS

Here are just a few statistics found in North American national surveys in 2014:
- According to the FBI, the rate of violent crimes in the United States from 2005–2014 was down by 16.2 percent
- In 2014, the FBI found that 68.9 percent of all crimes were committed by white offenders and 28.3 percent were by black or African-American offenders
- In 2014, Statistics Canada reported that 68 percent of all Canadians felt the police were doing a good job at treating people fairly.

POLICING AND PROFILES

The police are there to prevent crime and enforce the law. By its very nature, policing is a difficult and challenging job. It has varied greatly over the years, and from nation to nation. In many countries and societies, there are sometimes complex and difficult relationships between police and different ethnic groups.

Police and community

In some areas, the police can be a community-based force, made up of regular citizens acting on behalf of the public. Some believe that, to prevent or lessen crime, police officers need to be involved in the community—knowing people on the street, and understanding all sections of the community.

The Black Lives Matter movement was created in 2012, following the death of Trayvon Martin and aquittal of George Zimmerman. Members believe that black people are often targeted by law enforcers, and advocate for the liberation of black people from racism and violence.

Protests and riots broke out in the streets of Ferguson, Missouri, and other American cities after Darren Wilson, a police officer who shot and killed unarmed teenager Michael Brown, was not **indicted** for any criminal charges.

A war against crime

In some countries, police forces act as political agents of the state, taking part in a "war" against crime. If the police take on gangs or organized crime, things can turn violent. "Hard" policing, or the use of confrontation and force, may be needed, but it is not effective unless it is fair and transparent. Over-**authoritarian** or corrupt policing can be harmful, especially if members of the force include racists.

Biases that categorize certain groups of people as being more violent or of a lesser social class breeds resentment and dangerous beliefs about race. It criminalizes innocent people. One incident

"A riot is the language of the unheard."

Dr. Martin Luther King, Jr.

can set off a riot that can ruin community relations.

These issues are at the forefront of debates around the world. In the United Kingdom, judge Lord Scarman spoke about the "complex political, social, and economic issues" surrounding race, crime, and policing. He highlighted the police's lack of consultation with the community, excessive "stop and frisk" campaigns (see page 16), and the presence of racist officers in organizations.

"Instead of feeling protected by police, many African Americans are intimidated and live in daily fear that their children will face abuse, arrest and death at the hands of police officers..."

Statement by Sociologists for Justice, 2014

DOES "STOP AND FRISK" WORK?

If statistics demonstrate that ethnicity plays a role in certain criminal activities, does it make sense for police officers to pull over people from those ethnic groups and question them? Such activity is called racial profiling, and in some countries it is illegal. Why?

Racial profiling

Racial profiling means that law enforcers stop or target individuals solely based on their race. Without genuine grounds for suspicion, it should not be acceptable to stop people just because of their racial appearance. Doing so relies on a kind of prejudgment, or prejudice. Racial profiling encourages thinking in terms of racial stereotypes, and can contribute to the feeling of some ethnic groups that they are being unfairly targeted.

DEBATE   Is "stop and frisk" effective?

YES

It makes a difference. In 2013, a New York judge banned a "stop and frisk" program as being racist and unconstitutional. *In the month that followed, illegal shootings were up by nearly 13 percent and gun seizures fell by nearly 20 percent.*

NO

Many studies have shown that stop-and-frisk practices do not help reduce crime. Instead, they support stereotypes about ethnicity and crime, and increase feelings of resentment toward police in some communities, where some ethnic groups feel harassed by police.

Campaigners say that deliberately targeting people based on their race only makes the situation worse, damaging relationships between the community and the police.

Counterproductive?

As conflicts occur, community relations are damaged. Racial profiling has often been blamed for triggering city riots. African-American comedians have joked about the crime of "driving while black," because of how frequently African American and black Americans are stopped by police.

Checks and balances

In the United Kingdom, the *Police and Criminal Evidence Act* (PACE) was brought in to regulate the balance between police powers and public freedoms. It states that a police officer must have reasonable grounds of suspicion to stop and frisk. It also states that the person stopped has the right to complain. Although these are helpful regulations, they may not stop those who still abuse the system.

In many other countries and regions, people and organizations are speaking out against stop-and-frisk practices as well as other areas of policing. In the United States, many people believe that police officers should wear cameras to record the interactions they have with the people they stop.

Campaigners in New York are shown calling for an "end to racial profiling," by demonstrating against police techniques that appear to target people from certain racial groups.

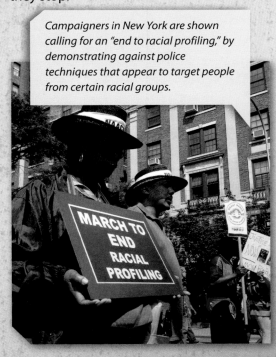

MARCH TO END RACIAL PROFILING

CRIMES OF HATRED

Considerations about race can be applied, whether appropriately or not, to any type of crime. However, some crimes are bred through racism itself, targeting specific people or groups based on their ethnicity. These are considered **hate crimes**.

Racist attacks

Racism can come in varying forms, from everyday incidents or rudeness and bullying to violent crime. All are harmful. To the person on the receiving end of "everyday racism," jokes and comments— even when the intent is not negative—can be depressing and humiliating.

Verbal abuse can soon become physical abuse, and a racist attack can become a murder. In North America, hate crimes have occurred throughout history. From the brutal killings of black people during times of slavery to anti-Muslim violence today, racism results in immense damage.

In 2013, members of the Tamil community in Ottawa, Canada in 2013 call for an end to attacks against Tamil citizens in Sri Lanka. Tamils are an ethnic group in Sri Lanka who have been killed and persecuted by the country's Sinhalese population for decades.

Crimes against humanity

Horrific crimes such as **human trafficking**, work **exploitation**, and slavery are sometimes based on race or ethnicity. In such cases, victims are not regarded as equal human beings, but as property or commodities to be exploited.

The worst racial crimes of all are known as crimes against humanity. They include "ethnic cleansing"—a hateful term first used in Serbia in 1992. It refers to the enforced removal of a whole ethnic group from a territory by destroying their homes and intimidating them through rape, violence, **deportation**, and murder. Genocide is murder on a large scale. It is the deliberate eradication, or destruction, of thousands or millions of people because of their ethnicity.

The **Holocaust** Memorial in Berlin, Germany, was built to commemorate the lives of Jews, Slavs, Roma, and other groups murdered during the genocide committed by the Nazi regime in WWII.

"**No one is born hating another person because of the color of his skin, or his background, or his religion. People must learn to hate, and if they can learn to hate, they can be taught to love, for love comes more naturally to the human heart than its opposite.**"

Nelson Mandela in his autobiography, *Long Walk to Freedom*, 1994

BIRMINGHAM, UNITED KINGDOM, 2013

Pavlo Lapshyn was a PhD student who won a competition in 2011 for a sponsored work placement with a software company in Birmingham, United Kingdom. Little did his employers know that Lapshyn was a white supremacist with a hatred of Muslims.

NEWS FLASH

Location: Birmingham, United Kingdom
Date: April 29, 2013
Incident: Homicide and bombing
Perpetrator: Pavlo Lapshyn (aged 25)
Victim: Mohammed Saleem (aged 82)
Outcome: Convicted

Mohammed Saleem (left) was the victim of a hate crime by racist killer Pavlo Lapshyn.

Mission of hatred

Just five days after arriving in Birmingham from his home in Dnipropetrovsk, Ukraine, Lapshyn followed Mohammed Saleem, a much-loved grandfather, as he left the mosque after evening prayers. Lapshyn stabbed the 82-year-old man to death a few yards from his home. The crime was recorded on a surveillance camera, but the image of the killer was not very clear,

> ## "My Dad was a well-loved man. He was respected by everyone in this community. We all have the right to feel safe and nobody should have to go through this... It is just unbearable, unbelievable."

Shazia Khan, Mohammed Saleem's daughter, on *BBC News*

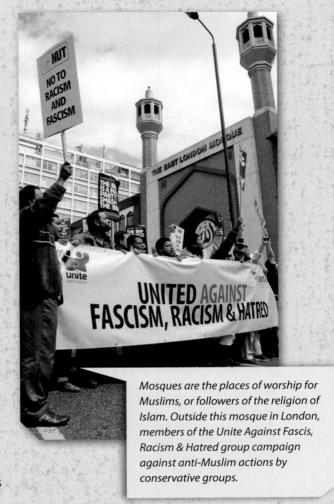

Mosques are the places of worship for Muslims, or followers of the religion of Islam. Outside this mosque in London, members of the Unite Against Fascis, Racism & Hatred group campaign against anti-Muslim actions by conservative groups.

and the attacker was hard to identify.

In June and July 2013, Lapshyn placed three homemade bombs outside mosques in nearby cities. Luckily, none of the bombs caused any injuries.

A life term

The police finally traced the crimes back to Pavlo Lapshyn. Equipment and computer files found in his home showed that he was a bomb-maker and racist, who believed white people were superior to others and wished to create racial conflict in the communities he had attacked. In October 2013, Lapshyn was sentenced to life in prison for the murder of Mohammed Saleem and for plotting to cause the explosions at the mosques.

> ## "You were motivated to commit the offences by religious and racial hatred in the hope that you would ignite racial conflict..."

The Honorable Mr Justice Sweeney presiding over Lapshyn's case

WHAT CAUSES RACIST CRIME?

Racist crime is often the result of a lack of understanding of other people and their cultures. Ignorance can lead to fear and anger, and even simple differences can cause friction. Sometimes, immigrants in communities feel unwelcome. This might cause them to be unable to understand local customs or learn new languages, creating more tension on both sides.

Scapegoating the innocent

After terrorist attacks or during a war, ethnic communities may find themselves scapegoated, or unfairly blamed, for acts of violence that had nothing to do with them. This happened to many Asians and Muslims after the September 11 attacks in New York City, Washington, DC, and Pennsylvania in 2001, when many people feared members of the ethnic group that had committed the attacks. Racist crime cannot be prevented by legislation alone. Social barriers and mistrust must be broken down with communication, education, and cooperation.

Fear of outsiders

In some situations, people fear that more

These demonstrators in Minneapolis protest against anti-Muslim attacks in the United States following the September 11, 2001 terrorist attacks.

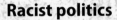

Greek students demonstrate in central Athens against the neo-Nazi Golden Dawn party in September 2013.

immigrants will mean more job competition. Economic rivalry, or the competition for jobs and money, is a common cause of ethnic tension and racist crime, even though immigration can actually be of benefit to an economy. Economic rivalries throughout history have caused communities to fear ethnic groups.

Racist politics

Instead of trying to heal wounds, some political parties try to win power by playing on these public fears. In Greece, the **neo-Nazi** Golden Dawn party has attacked and murdered African and Asian immigrants and **asylum seekers**. In 2013, the Greek government declared the party a criminal organization. However, Golden Dawn had 21 seats in parliament, which were fairly won in an election. If the people elect racist criminals to represent them, how should a democratic government respond?

> "[Golden Dawn is] a criminal organization that tried to cover itself under a political cloak."
>
> Simos Kedikoglou, spokesperson for the Greek government

DEBATE Do people have the right to make a racist speech in public?

YES
You may agree or disagree with what a speaker has to say, but freedom of speech should be protected by the law.

NO
Hate speech may invite violent crime, and racists should not be given the chance to destroy community relations.

RACISM IN THE SYSTEM

A criminal justice system may police individual **bigotry** or the violence of a racist political party. However, forms of racism can also be embedded in the whole political or legal system. It can exist in government, education, health care, or big corporations.

Collective failure

This kind of racism is called institutional racism. A widely used definition of the term comes from Sir William Macpherson, who spoke on it after the racially-motivated murder of a 19-year-old black teenager. Macpherson explains institutional racism as "the collective failure of an organization to provide an appropriate and professional service to people because of their color, culture, or ethnic origin." Macpherson called for education and procedures in the United Kingdom to be revised to discourage racism, and for the recruitment of more police officers from different ethnic groups.

Cécile Kyenge became Italy's first black minister in 2013. Since her appointment, she has faced racist abuse from right-wing organizations, and even from politicians.

Racism in government

Many countries have legislation in place to prevent institutional racism, however it is often treated lightly by the courts or ignored by individuals. Sometimes whole areas of government policy are designed to exclude people, such as restricting immigration or civil rights on grounds of race or religion.

Sometimes, racism defines a government and its law. This can be called constitutional racism. From 1948 to 1994, the government of South Africa enforced a policy called apartheid—the segregation of society by race. The racist policies of Nazi rule in Germany from 1933 to 1945, which resulted in the Holocaust, were built into the governance of the nation. A racist constitution turns justice on its head, turning opponents of racism into criminals.

According to the United States Census Bureau in 2010, these were the following percentages of self-identified ethnicities in some positions of power:

Chief Executives and Legislators
84.4% White
4.5% Hispanic or Latino
3.3% Black
4.4 % Asian
0.4% Native American or Alaskan Native

Police Officers
70% White
12.5% Hispanic or Latino
12.4% Black
2% Asian
0.7% Native American or Alaskan Native

These numbers show that white people hold more positions of power than other ethnicities, suggesting that there is institutional racism.

In May 2009, immigrants and their supporters marched to the White House in Washington, DC, on International Workers' Day, to protest against what they consider to be racist raids by the police on their workplaces.

CANADA, 1980–2016

North America has a long history of institutional racism, in the way that Native peoples were treated with the coming of white settlers. For these groups, white settlement meant loss of land, violence, discrimination, enforced resettlement, and refusal of civil rights.

NEWS FLASH

Location: Canada
Date: 1980-2016
Incident: Murders of First Nations, Métis, and Inuit women
Issue: Lack of authoritative action
Victims: More than 1,000 missing and murdered First Nations, Métis, and Inuit women
Outcome: National inquiry

Demonstrators protest outside Parliament in Ottawa, Ontario, for the government to take action for the missing and murdered women.

Missing and murdered women

In 2014, the Royal Canadian Mounted Police (RCMP) conducted a report that examined an issue identified by **Amnesty International** in 2004: a disproportionate number of First Nations, Métis, and Inuit women in Canada were experiencing violence. The RCMP report concluded that 1,181 Native women and girls had been murdered or reported missing since 1980—many of these cases being unsolved. Often born into extreme poverty with limited resources for help, Native women are particularly vulnerable to violence.

Groups such as the United Nations and the Native Women's Association of Canada, as well as the general public, have criticized Canadian authorities and the government for their failure to prevent this violence, and their lack of effort in investigating the cases. Some argue the situation is an example of institutional racism, since Native peoples are often labeled by authorities as perpetrators rather than victims. In 2015, the Canadian government began a national inquiry into the deaths and disappearances.

Bringing realities to light

Many people feel that the high number of missing and murdered Native women and girls is part of a larger issue in Canada. Due to a long history of abuse against Native peoples, including **residential schools**, land seizures, and **disenfranchisement**, Native peoples in Canada are subjected to racism, poverty, and lack of opportunity. Many reservations, or land allocated to Native peoples, do not have living necessities such as clean water and adequate housing. Native communities have high rates of suicide and violence. The UN has called on the Canadian government to solve these problems.

> # STATISTICS AND FIGURES
>
> Native women make up about 4 percent of the female population in Canada, but were 16 percent of women murdered between 1980 and 2012.
>
> The suicide rate on reserves is up to five times higher than the national rate.
>
> Native women are 3.5 times more likely to experience violence than non-Native women in Canada.

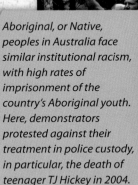

Aboriginal, or Native, peoples in Australia face similar institutional racism, with high rates of imprisonment of the country's Aboriginal youth. Here, demonstrators protested against their treatment in police custody, in particular, the death of teenager TJ Hickey in 2004.

"...Indigenous people [are] being over-policed but under-protected."

Amnesty International Report, *Stolen Sisters*, 2004

HOW CAN WE TACKLE RACISM?

Most cities are multicultural. That means they are home to people from many ethnic backgrounds who have different faiths and speak different languages. How might we tackle institutional racism so that all community members have fair and equal chances at success?

Values and rules

Some people believe that the best way of diffusing tensions is to celebrate the diversity of all people and campaign for equality within communities. This policy is called multiculturalism, which means that the area embraces a diverse set of cultural attitudes and traditions. However, others argue that multiculturalism reinforces social divisions. They think that it is better for all people in a community to live under a single set of values and practices. Another way to combat institutional racism is to reverse the process of racial discrimination. This policy, called affirmative action, or employment equity, ensures that people from all ethnic groups are represented across a wide range of employment.

Campaigners demonstrate in support of immigrant rights in Washington, DC. The United States is a country with a long history of immigration.

My Faith, My Vote for Immigration Reform

28

Affirmative action can mean that companies or institutions, such as schools, will reserve spaces to be filled by people of certain ethnicities and genders. This means that a diverse population is well represented.

Who stands for law and order?

People with racist views often claim that they stand for the betterment of their nations, saying that ethnic groups do not belong there. They ignore the fact that many members of those communities were actually born in the country. The world is made up of migrants.

Racist policies do not make their countries better. Nations that depend on slavery, apartheid, or injustice are unsustainable economically, morally, and politically, and risk collapse. Institutional racism also extends past the national level. Some argue that the global economy favors the richer Western nations over less developed nations, leaving many to live in extreme poverty. They argue for a unified, global economy that treats all regions fairly.

DEBATE

Is affirmative action the best way to tackle institutional racism?

YES

Filling an agreed quota of positions with a certain number of people from different ethnic groups repairs imbalances and challenges deeply ingrained racial stereotypes.

NO

It takes away the basic right of equal opportunities for all. The only measure for recruitment should be finding the best person for the job. That benefits everybody.

THE ROLE OF THE MEDIA

The media has a lot of power in the way we think about crime and race. People who have little personal experience of crime find out about these issues in the news. Media sources such as newspapers and television shape the impressions and opinions of the public. Politicians can gain votes by tailoring their policies to match public opinion.

Media hype

Some media sources offer valuable insights or investigations into issues of race and crime, but many use a sensationalist treatment of the news. Reporting news in a sensationalist way is to exaggerate stories about crime or terrorism to evoke fear, anger, and other emotions in the public. This is often done because it sells newspapers or brings in viewers, but it often gives misleading impressions about crime—that crime is rising when it is not, for example, or that certain groups are at risk.

Journalists' use of language can exaggerate situations, contributing to a "**climate of fear**," in which people are made to be suspicious or fearful of certain groups perceived to be committing crimes. You might often hear the words

Some politicians that have anti-immigration policies, such as Donald Trump, benefit from sensationalist reports about immigration and crime. Here, a demonstrator holds signs in Washington, DC, outside the building where Trump was speaking on foreign policy during the 2016 US presidential race.

"crime wave" or "flood of immigrants." Both suggest that something is threatening, overwhelming, or dangerous.

Stereotyping

Crime reports are often framed in terms of race, without going into other issues that may be just as relevant. This distorts the viewer's or reader's knowledge of the crime, and reinforces the idea that some ethnic groups are predisposed, or likely, to commit crime. Often, people seeking safety in another country are not presented as refugees desperately fleeing war or persecution in their own land, but as unwelcome foreigners or criminals that impose on host countries.

Media trucks are shown gathered outside the Criminal Justice Center in Sanford, Florida, to cover the events following the shooting of Trayvon Martin by George Zimmerman (see pages 10–11).

THINK ABOUT IT

In 2013, a news article written by Brian Ross was published in the *Huffington Post*, with the title "Why Two White Kids Are a Senseless Tragedy but an Arab American is Terrorism."

The article looked at how the media portrays the perpetrators of crimes. Ross focused on the language used by the media to describe perpetrators of different races. He wrote,

"Most of what was covered, was the [white shooters'] mental state and what mental defect drives kids from white suburbia to shoot their fellow students. [...] white shooters get psych profiles. Non-white shooters get family backgrounds, and, in the case of Maj. Hasan, stretches to link to terrorism. Apparently you cannot just be mentally disturbed and Arab-American or South Korean."

Why might the media imply that an Arab-American perpetrator is a "terrorist," but describe white perpetrators as troubled and mentally ill? Does this make sense? Why or why not?

FRANCE AND KOSOVO, 2013

Roma, or Romani, people are a group that is traditionally nomadic. Roma people have been persecuted in various countries throughout history, and many have fled to western Europe. In 2013, France's Interior Minister Manuel Valls declared that Roma people were "incompatible with the French way of life." He ordered the eviction of about 10,000 Roma from temporary camps in France.

NEWS FLASH

Location: Doubs, France, and Mitrovica, Kosovo
Date: October 9, 2013
Incident: Expulsion of Roma family
Issues: Deportation and the law
Immigrant: Leonarda Dibrani (aged 15, left)
Outcome: Deportation

Following their expulsion from France, Leonarda and her family returned to Kosovo, a country still recovering from war.

The girl on the bus

The topic of illegal immigration became one of the biggest stories in the French media in 2013. Many believed, and were supported by French lawmakers, that Roma people had not legally immigrated into the country and therefore should be forcefully deported. That October, a Roma family living in eastern France was expelled from the home they had lived in for 5 years. When the police came for them, 15-year-old Leonarda Dibrani was away on a school trip. The police tracked her down and took her off the bus in full view of her friends. The family was deported to Kosovo.

Supporters and opponents

Many people were upset by the harsh way the teenager had been dealt with. School children and students protested on the streets against the seizure of Leonarda Dibrani.

However, other people applauded any crackdown on illegal migrants. The French government insisted it had behaved humanely. It offered to take Leonarda back to be reassessed, but not the rest of her family. She declined the offer. Later, an official report by the government supported the deportation of the Dibrani family as being legitimate.

"**There are bad refugees in France who get papers easily—we didn't do anything bad. They did it to us because we are Roma. We would be treated differently if our skin was a different color.**"

Reshat Dibrani, Leonarda's father

Many French people have been concerned about the number of refugees coming to France. Some parts of the media link these refugees with begging and even crime.

CAN THE MEDIA BE RACIST?

Reports in newspapers, on television, and on the Internet influence the ways in which we view people. It is important to look for bias in newscasts and in entertainment. The ways in which different ethnic groups are portrayed in real life and in fictional settings can have profound effects on how they are perceived—and even how they perceive themselves.

Tunnel-vision TV

The views of people in power, such as senior police officers, judges, and politicians, influence what is shown in the media about a crime because they control or create the information made available to the public. This often limits what media sources are able to cover. It also often excludes the voices of people who are **disempowered**, such as the victims of crime. This limited reporting can encourage stereotyping, as well as xenophobia, which is the fear or hatred of people from other countries. For example, news from Africa or Asia tends to focus on famine, natural disasters, war, or terrorism—not the many positive stories about their everyday lives and cultures. This helps build an impression that people living there are always at risk or involved in crime, and are not contributing members of their societies.

Although media stories about African countries often emphasize violence, war, famine, or other issues, local people, such as these schoolchildren in Zambia, go about their lives in similar ways to us.

On-screen bias

The image of different ethnic groups presented in television, movies, and in computer games has a powerful effect on how members of these groups are viewed by others, and how they might see themselves. On-screen criminals, for example, are often played by non-white actors, while a movie's hero is usually a white male. It is important to think about the biases or stereotypes that may be present in the TV shows or movies we watch. We should be aware of the over- or under-representation of certain races in particular roles and understand how this might influence our views. Does the media distort or exaggerate their lives or experiences for ratings and profit?

> ## "People of color have a constant frustration of not being represented, or being misrepresented, and these images go around the world."
>
> **African-American filmmaker Spike Lee**

"Gangsta" rap

Popular music has a history of being associated with race and crime by some politicians, law enforcement officials, and journalists. For example, the lyrics of hip hop and gangsta rap have long been accused of promoting guns, knives, drug abuse, violence, rape, and aggression toward some communities. Those who defend the music insist it reflects the society in which it has its roots. For some artists, music can make a political statement that draws attention to the difficult conditions in their communities.

American rapper 50 Cent has been accused of promoting gun violence through his lyrics and music. He rejects this accusation, saying that music is a mirror and his lyrics reflect his own life experiences growing up in a poor neighborhood.

FERGUSON, 2014

On August 9, 2014, Michael Brown was fatally shot by Darren Wilson, a Ferguson police officer. He had stolen cigars from a local convenience store and was walking down the street, when Wilson attempted to stop him for the crime. Witness accounts differ widely about what happened next, but what we do know is that Brown—an unarmed black teenager—was killed. His death, and the fact that officer Darren Wilson was not indicted, caused a national uproar.

NEWS FLASH

Location: Ferguson, St. Louis, Missouri
Date: August 9, 2014
Incident: Shooting of Michael Brown
Issues: Police violence, media bias, racism, and rioting
Outcome: Non-indictment of Darren Wilson

A crowd gathered to create a memorial for Michael Brown at the site where he was killed.

Hands up?

According to some witnesses, Brown had his hands up in surrender at the time that he was shot. This influenced protestors to use the slogan "Hands up, Don't shoot" in their campaigns against police violence. Other witnesses claim that Brown had been advancing threateningly toward Wilson. Evidence showed Brown was facing Wilson when he was shot, supporting this claim. Wilson was not charged for his death—a decision that many feel is unjust. Although the circumstances are controversial, what remains is the widespread debate that was sparked as a result of the tragic event.

The killing of Michael Brown sparked a debate about police brutality and racism. Many people felt that Wilson should have been arrested for murder. Activists cited other instances of police violence against black and African-American citizens, including the death of Eric Garner in New York.

Black Lives Matter

When Darren Wilson was not charged with any crime, many people began to speak out about the experience of being a black person in the United States. The Black Lives Matter movement, founded after the death of Trayvon Martin, gained more media attention. The movement claims that, because of a long history of racism—including slavery—in the country, black lives are not considered as valuable as others, a theory supported by the lack of convictions against their killers in some high-profile cases.

Media coverage

Activists and the general public noted that, in news coverage of the shooting, the media had chosen to circulate images of Brown in "street" clothing, flashing a peace sign which some media outlets claimed was a gang symbol. Some argued that, by showing this image, the media was trying to imply that Brown was a threatening, dangerous man rather than a teenager who had just graduated high school. It's important to consider how the images and words chosen by news outlets can show biased reporting.

> **"...the narrative the media paints surrounding black people in America more often than not includes depicting us as violent thugs with gang and drug affiliations."**
>
> Yesha Callahan, *The Root*, 2014

JUSTICE FOR ALL

The principles of racial equality have inspired an international framework of law. The Universal Declaration of Human Rights (UDHR) was drawn up by the UN in 1948. This was the first global expression of the essential qualities needed by all humans—of every ethnicity—to lead a safe and positive life.

Without distinction of any kind...

Article after article of the UDHR tackles the issues of racism and justice head on. It affirms the equality of all people, in society and before the law. Later international conventions addressed aspects of racism in more detail—genocide, the treatment of refugees, discrimination in employment, civil rights, the rights of Native peoples, and the rights of migrant workers. The document reads, "Everyone is entitled to all the rights and freedoms set forth in this Declaration, without distinction of any kind, such as race, color, sex, language, religion, political or other opinion, national or social origin, property, birth or other status."

The UN defines apartheid as "inhuman acts committed for the purpose of establishing and maintaining domination by one racial group of persons over any other racial group of persons and systematically oppressing them."

People gathered in Washington, DC, in August 2013 to commemorate the 50th anniversary of a historic civil rights march led by activist Martin Luther King, Jr., who called for equality for all people.

The rule of law

Even though the desire to abolish slavery has endured since the 1800s, national laws vary widely from one country or state to another. This has made change difficult to achieve, as campaign groups have to deal with different legislation from one country to the next. Milestones were reached in the 1960s, achieved by civil rights campaigns in the United States and the first anti-racist legislation in Europe. Legislation since then has made efforts to remedy issues of institutional racism. In Canada, the *Multiculturalism Act* promotes participation of all cultures in Canadian society. Britain's *Equality Act* of 2010 requires institutions to plan for equality in employment, services, and budgeting.

Stand up for your rights!

These laws wouldn't be passed if people did not speak out for their rights. There is still a long way to go. It takes a lot of courage to speak out against racism in our communities, schools, or workplaces, but it is a challenge that each new generation must take on.

TURKEY AND SYRIA, 2015

Syria is a country in the Middle East. In recent years, it has been ravaged by a civil war between an oppressive government, rebels attempting to overthrow it, and outside groups such as the terrorist group **ISIL**. Millions of Syrian people have had to leave their homes— including one particular family who fled temporarily to Turkey. On September 2, 2015, the Kurdi family attempted to reach Europe by boat.

NEWS FLASH

Location: On the coast of Turkey
Date: September 2, 2015
Incident: Shipwreck of refugees
Issues: Human smuggling, border controls, refugees
Victims: 3-year-old Alan Kurdi, his brother and mother, and 2 other refugees
Outcome: 5 deaths, convictions of smugglers

A memorial was held for 3-year-old Alan Kurdi on the beach where his body was discovered on September 2.

The human smugglers

To get to safety, desperate refugees sometimes must pay large sums of money to criminal gangs, who guide them through deserts and across seas and smuggle them across borders. On the way, the refugees may be robbed, raped, beaten, or taken hostage. The Kurdi family had allegedly paid thousands of dollars to smugglers to get them to the Greek island of Kos.

A tragedy at sea

On September 2, 2015, a small rubber boat set off in the dark of night from Turkey. The boat was filled far over its capacity and capsized after about five minutes. Five of the refugees on board drowned. That morning, a Turkish photographer came across little Alan Kurdi's lifeless body on the Turkish shore. The image she took of him was circulated through the media, raising

...rally in Toronto, ...ntario in November ...015 sends a message ...f welcome to Syrian ...fugees. The ...monstrators held ...gns to combat ...ti-refugee sentiment.

horror and outrage around the world. The image also drew attention to the Syrian refugee crisis. Millions of people are **displaced** by civil war in Syria, but have limited places to seek safety. Since the Kurdi family was attempting to reach Europe, and allegedly Canada afterward, the tragedy made many Western countries reexamine their immigration policies.

The plight of asylum seekers

An insecure world, a global economy, and economic injustice have placed refugees and asylum seekers at the center of a political storm. Those who do manage to settle in new countries are often treated like the worst criminals, insulted in the media, subjected to racist abuse, or even attacked on the streets.

The smugglers who orchestrated the Kurdi's failed attempt were sentenced to four years in prison, but are there others to blame? The illegal migrants who drowned in search of a better life? The perpetrators of civil war who forced them to flee Syria? Or the politicians who decide border policy and access to the European Union or other Western countries, including Canada and the United States?

"...we have fallen into a globalized indifference."

Pope Francis, Head of the Roman Catholic Church, 2013

CAN THERE EVER BE JUSTICE?

How can the biggest race crimes, such as apartheid or genocide, ever be resolved? Can the racist attitudes fueled by these crimes ever be changed? Can there ever be meaningful justice for the millions who have been murdered in the name of "ethnic cleansing" or "racial purity"?

Trials and tribunals

Sometimes perpetrators of crimes against humanity are held accountable. At the end of the second World War in 1945, Nazis responsible for the murder of millions of Jews in the Holocaust were tried at Nuremberg in Germany.

After the Yugoslav Wars of 1991 to 1999, a number of Serbians were tried at a UN **tribunal**. They were charged with the racist crime of ethnic cleansing.

International prosecutions

Since 2002, crimes against humanity can be tried at the International Criminal Court (ICC) at The Hague in Netherlands. Many ICC cases have investigated ethnic crimes in Africa, such as those alleged to have taken place in Darfur since 2003. Some nations say the ICC is ignoring crimes committed by Western leaders. Others have criticized the United States and Israel for not signing on as members of the ICC.

The International Criminal Tribunal for the former Yugoslavia in The Hague, Netherlands, has overseen the trial of several people accused of war crimes during the Yugoslav Wars.

Reconciling difference

Restorative justice is another kind of process that aims to heal wounds and move forward. It restores the dignity of victims and sometimes offers an **amnesty** to the offenders rather than prosecuting and punishing them on points of law. From 1996, South Africa's Truth and Reconciliation Commission (TRC) attempted to remedy or compensate for the crimes of apartheid. Similar commissions have been held in many other nations, too, such as the Truth and Reconciliation Commission of Canada which sought to work through the crimes of residential schools—where Native children were abused and forced to give up their cultural heritage.

Archbishop Desmond Tutu was Chairman of South Africa's Truth and Reconciliation Commission, which used restorative justice in an attempt to heal the divide between citizens created by apartheid.

DEBATE

Can restorative justice remedy a crime against humanity?

YES

Offering restorative action can help victims find peace. It can also help to end cycles of violence between communities.

NO

If it does not convict perpetrators, and lets racists and criminals off the hook, it cannot really be called justice.

"**When we see others as the enemy, we risk becoming what we hate. When we oppress others, we end up oppressing ourselves. All of our humanity is dependent on recognizing the humanity in others.**"

Archbishop Desmond Tutu, chair of South Africa's Truth and Reconciliation Commission

STANDING TOGETHER

There is a popular saying that "there is only one race, the human race." When thinking this way, it's important to remember that our global history means that different groups of people are privileged, while others are disempowered. However, embracing the "human race" might mean that we realize that it is only peoples' ideas about "different" races that divides the world.

Who holds the power?

Racist ideals or criminal intent might be held by a human being of any ethnic group. However, the consequence of those ideas depends on who holds the power. Often, power lies with the majority who can make life miserable for minority groups. An imbalance of power in society can create areas that are underprivileged or poverty-stricken. Groups with too much political, social, military, or economic power can create laws of segregation, an apartheid government, or acts of genocide.

Who gets the jobs?

Equality cannot be sustained only by legislation. It cannot be created without economic opportunity. Black youths in the poorer districts of big cities deserve an alternative to gang cultures that override their communities—they need genuine, rewarding jobs. Racists often blame the high rate of young black offenders on race, rather than on economic and social conditions. They also often ignore the fact that it is usually black community activists who have been at the forefront of campaigning against gun and knife crime, and building trust between the community and law enforcers, such as the police.

The way forward

One person who challenged oppressive, racist power was Nelson Mandela (1918–2013). Mandela broke the law to take on South Africa's apartheid government, and served 27 years in jail. In the end, he defeated institutional racism with a vision of equality, education, and economic justice for all.

This metal sculpture of Nelson Mandela stands at the site where he was arrested by the apartheid government in 1962.

Everyone, no matter what their race, ethnicity, or community, can work together to bring about change. Together, people may begin to defuse the fear and rage that come from racism, stereotypes, and a lack of understanding.

"We are fighting for a society where people will cease thinking in terms of color."

Nelson Mandela

GLOSSARY

adaptation
When something or someone adjusts or changes to fit in with new environments

amnesty
A pardon granted by a governing body for an offense

Amnesty International
An international nonprofit organization that works to protect human rights

apartheid
A legal and political system that classifies and segregates people according to race or color; South Africa was governed under an apartheid system from 1948 to 1994.

assumption
Something that is taken for granted and believed to be true, even though it may be false or misleading

asylum seeker
Someone seeking refuge in another country; asylum seekers are usually fleeing political persecution, famine, or poverty

authoritarian
Describing a system in which individuals are expected to obey authority over their will

bigotry
Beliefs or opinions that are based on intolerance or prejudice, and shape people's thoughts and actions against other groups or individuals

climate of fear
The provoking of fear in the public to achieve political or economic goals

corporate tax evasion
A crime in which a corporation intentionally does not pay their required taxes

deportation
Removing a person or a group of individuals from a country by force and sending them to another country

descent
The connection between a person and their ancestors

disempowered
When a person or group has self-authority removed and is made weak or unimportant

disenfranchisement
Taking away someone's legal rights, especially the right to vote

disparities
Large, evident differences or inequalities

displaced
The act of being forced from one's home

ethnic
Describing a certain group with a common racial, national, social, cultural, or religious background

evolution
A gradual process of formation, development, or change that usually occurs in response to changing environmental conditions

exploitation
The unjust or immoral use of someone or something for personal gain

hate crimes
Offenses against a person committed

because of the offender's hate, prejudice, or bias against them—usually on the basis of race, ethnicity, religion, gender, etc.

Holocaust
The mass murder (genocide) carried out in Europe by Nazi Germany during the 1930s and 1940s. The victims included about six million Jews, as well as Roma, other eastern Europeans, and other groups such as disabled and homosexual people.

human trafficking
The illegal movement of people, most commonly for forced labor and sexual slavery

indictment
The official charging of a person for a crime, usually done by a jury

Indigenous
Referring to people who have lived in, or are native to, a region for a long time

institutional racism
Racist attitudes or inequality practiced within companies, governments, or public bodies, such as schools, colleges, or police forces

ISIL
Short for Islamic State of Iraq and the Levant (also called ISIS); a militant group that follows an extreme branch of Islam and is known for committing war crimes and crimes against humanity

Ku Klux Klan
A group of white Americans who believed whites were superior to other races, and who were extremely violent toward blacks, Jews, and other ethnic groups

neo-Nazi
A person or group of people that follow the racist beliefs of Hitler's Nazi regime

prejudice
A preconceived negative attitude that prevents fair judgment and leads to the unfair treatment of other people

race
Usually defined as a division of people in the human population that have similar physical characteristics, coming from common ancestry

residential schools
Government and church-run schools where Native children were forcibly taken from their homes in order to assimilate, or integrate, them into American and Canadian culture

Roma
One of several names used to describe the ethnic group also known as Romanies or "Gypsies," which is considered derogatory

statistics
Data, or numbers, that are collected, analyzed, presented, and studied

stereotyping
Having a simplified or generalized view on a group of people, that does not take individual characteristics into account

tribunal
A person, or group of people, that are given the authority to make judgments on disputes or claims

unconsitutional
Something that does not follow, or is contrary to, a country's constitution

INDEX